The Berenstain Bears
and the
BAD
INFLUENCE

When new friends get together
to have a little fun,
the result can spell *trouble*
for nearly everyone !

The Berenstain Bears

and the

BAD INFLUENCE

Stan & Jan Berenstain
with Mike Berenstain

HarperFestival®
A Division of HarperCollinsPublishers

One Saturday morning Sister Bear came home looking like a storm cloud. She stomped up the front steps, through the house, and into the kitchen.

"I'm never going to speak to that Lizzy Bruin again!" she declared.

"Oh, dear!" said Mama. "Lizzy must have done something pretty terrible."

"That's right," said Sister. "She invited me over to play Bearbies. It was supposed to be just the two of us. But when I got there, Anna, Muffie, and Jill were already there with their Bearbie dolls and there wasn't any room for mine."

"But, dear," said Mama, "it seems to me that you can't have too many friends."

"Yes," said Sister. "But Lizzy was my best friend, and you can only have one *best* friend at a time!" With that, she tossed her Bearbie tote to Mama and stomped back out.

Miranda Moss, who was about Sister's age, was in just as bad a mood as Sister. Miranda was new in the neighborhood. She and her family had just moved in around the corner from the Bear family.

Miranda didn't want to move. She was upset about it. She was upset about leaving her friends, her school, and her neighborhood.

"I know you're upset about moving, Miranda," said her mother. "But your father was transferred to the Beartown office and we had no choice. Now why don't you go out and have a look at your new neighborhood? Maybe you'll like it."

"I'll go out and have a look at it," said Miranda. "But I won't like it."

Sister was sitting on her front steps when Miranda came along.

"Hello," said Miranda.

"Hello, yourself," said Sister.

"I just moved in," said Miranda. "What's it like here?"

"It's not like anything," said Sister. "It's just a place."

Miranda looked around. "It's kinda quiet," she said.

"I guess," said Sister.

"A little too quiet," said Miranda with a grin.

Sister looked around. "Maybe it is," she said.

"Is that yours?" asked Miranda, pointing to Sister's big trike.

"Yep," said Sister.

"Maybe we could go for a little spin," said Miranda.
"You could show me around."

"Sure," said Sister, mounting the trike. "Hop on."
Miranda climbed on the back.

"Okay," said Sister. "Here we go!"

And off they went with Sister pedaling hard and Miranda
hanging on for dear life.

"Good," said Mama, looking out the window. "Sister has found a new friend."

"What's the matter with her old friends?" asked Papa, coming in from his shop for a cup of tea.

"Sister had a falling out with Lizzy Bruin. Nothing serious—just the usual sort of cub spat," said Mama as she watched the trike whiz by.

"Any good hills around here?" asked Miranda, hugging Sister a little tighter as she pedaled on.

"Lots," said Sister, "but Dead Bear's Hill is the best."

"Can we try it?" asked Miranda.

"Sure," said Sister. "It's this way. I know a shortcut we can take."

The trouble was that the shortcut was through Mizz McGrizz's tulips.

"Hiyo, cowbear!" cried Miranda.

"Yippee-yea!" cried Sister.

Mizz McGrizz was inside watering her begonias at the time and saw the whole thing from her window.

"My tulips!" she cried. "My beautiful tulips! One of those cubs looks like Sister Bear. Well, I just might give her mother a call."

Dead Bear's Hill was very high. Sister hesitated at the top. "That's Farmer Ben's place down there, " she said.

"I know," said Miranda. "We bought some vegetables from him this morning. *Well*?"

"Well, what?" said Sister.

"Are we going to go down Dead Bear's Hill *or not*?" asked Miranda.

"I've gone down on a sled lots of times," said Sister. "But I've never gone down on wheels."

"There's always gotta be a first time," said Miranda.

"Okay," said Sister, taking her feet off the pedals. "Here we go-o-o-o-o-o!"

The trouble was that there was a curve at the bottom of Dead Bear's Hill and they didn't quite make it. They rolled into Farmer Ben's orchard, and into one of his apple trees. They knocked down quite a few apples.

"Are you hurt?" asked Miranda.

"I don't think so," said Sister.

"Hey, these look like pretty nice apples," said Miranda.

"We're supposed to stay away from Ben's apples," said Sister, "but since these are already on the ground . . ."

"They'll just rot," said Miranda. They scooped up some apples and put them in their pockets.

"Hey, how about you pedaling for a while?" said Sister.

"Fine with me," said Miranda. And off they rode, munching apples.

Farmer Ben was feeding his chickens at the time. He didn't know how it happened—all he saw were cubs loading up on his apples. "Why, that's Sister Bear and that new cub. Well, their mothers are going to hear from me!"

"What's that big thing parked in the road?" asked Miranda, pedaling on at Sister's direction.

"That's Grizzly Gus's cement mixer," said Sister. "He must be doing some work."

"Maybe we can write our names in the wet cement," said Miranda. The trouble was that they were already riding through it.

"Pedal harder!" cried Sister. "Steer for the woods!"

Grizzly Gus was jumping up and down and waving his cement smoother. "That looked like Sister Bear and that new Moss cub," said Grizzly Gus. He reached for his cell phone.

"I know a back way home," said Sister. "But we'll have to cross Mud Creek on those stepping stones."

But the stones were for stepping, not riding. They fell in. It wasn't deep, but it sure was muddy. They pulled themselves out and headed for home.

All in all it had been quite a Saturday morning.

The phones in the tree
house and the Mosses' house
were ringing off the hook.

"Yes, Mizz McGrizz, this is
Mama Bear. Sister Bear and
another cub? Your tulips? Oh, dear!
Hmm, I think I know what's going
on, and I'll certainly deal with it.
Thank you for your call.

"Well," said Mama, turning to
Papa. "I was pleased when Sister
found a new friend, but it's
perfectly clear that this new
friend is a bad influence."

RING

Meanwhile over at the Moss house, Mrs. Moss was on the phone with Farmer Ben. "Miranda and a cub named Sister Bear stole your apples? Oh, dear! I think I know what's going on, and I'll certainly take care of it.

"Well," said Mrs. Moss, turning to Mr. Moss. "Miranda seems to have found a new friend. But unfortunately this new friend is a very bad influence."

RING

At the tree house Mama Bear answered the phone again.

"Yes, Gus, this is Mama Bear. Rode through your wet cement? Sister and another cub? How awful. I'm truly sorry, Gus. But I think I know what's going on, and I'll certainly deal with it."

And to Papa she added, "That new cub is an even worse influence than I thought. Sister's not to have anything more to do with her."

Mrs. Moss was just as upset about Sister as Mama was about Miranda.

"I gather this *new friend* is a cub named Sister Bear," said Mrs. Moss. "I'm going to call and complain to her mother."

"Now, I wouldn't do that, my dear," cautioned Mr. Moss. "Not until . . . " But Mrs. Moss had placed the call.

"Hmm," she said. "The line's busy."

It was busy because Mama was trying to call Mrs. Moss to complain about Miranda.

Just then Sister came in the front door.

"My goodness!" said Mama. "You're a mess!"

"Yeah, we fell into Mud Creek trying to ride across. But it's just mud. It'll come off," said Sister with a grin.

"You certainly seem a lot happier now," said Mama.

"That's because I have a new best friend," said Sister. "Her name is Miranda."

"That's something I want to talk to you about, dear," said Mama. "You and this Miranda seem to have been having quite a time. I've had a number of angry calls this morning. I'm afraid this Miranda is what you call a *bad influence* and I don't want you playing with her anymore."

"That's not fair!" protested Sister. "It was my fault, too. I was just as much a bad influence on her as she was on me! Besides, we didn't get into trouble on purpose. It was kind of an accident."

"Well, you two are going to have to make things right with your neighbors," explained Mama.

Sister Bear and Miranda had a very busy afternoon. After planting some new bulbs in Mizz McGrizz's tulip patch, they stopped by and explained about the apples to Farmer Ben.

Then they apologized to Grizzly Gus for messing up his
new cement. He was very nice about it. He even let them write
their initials in a corner of the smoothed-out wet cement.

The next day, Sister not only made up with
Lizzy, Anna, Muffie, and Jill, she introduced
Miranda to the gang. After all, it was just as
Mama said: "You can't have too many friends."